For my father.
— J.-F. D.

I AM A BEAR

JEAN-FRANÇOIS DUMONT

EERDMANS BOOKS FOR YOUNG READERS

GRAND RAPIDS, MICHIGAN • CAMBRIDGE, U.K.

I don't know how I got here . . .
I have no memory of my life before,
just a few images that flash
before my eyes from time to time,
like the car headlights that
sweep over my bed at night.
All I know is that one morning
I woke up here, on this street,
and I haven't left it since.

I am a bear.

I know, there's no such thing as
a bear who lives on the street,
right in the middle of everyone.
It took me a while to admit it too.
At first I thought that I was like everyone else:
I'd go home at night for dinner
and fall asleep peacefully in a nice soft bed.
But I quickly realized that that life wasn't for us bears.
That's why I sleep here, on these cardboard boxes, on the street.

At first, I didn't know that I was a bear.
But when I tried to speak to this little lady
who was passing by, and I saw her reaction,
I started to understand.

Apparently,
bears do not communicate well
with people.

I tried again, of course.

The woman at the bakery fainted,
the doorman at No. 9 called the police,
and the butcher chased me to the end
of the street with his big sharp knife.
Fortunately, bears run faster than butchers.
Since then, I've learn to keep quiet,
and in spite of my big body,
I make myself as small as possible.

Finding something to eat hasn't been very easy,
even though there's no shortage of food!
Rolls and chocolate-filled pastries in the bakery window,
beef ribs, sausage, and smoked bacon at the butcher shop,
jars of jam and honey on the grocer's shelves —
it's all enough to make your mouth water.

But when I tried to help myself, the big paw of a security guard came down on my shoulder. Without really understanding what was happening to me, I found myself outside, facedown on the sidewalk, my stomach still empty. I realized that it was better to pick through the garbage cans at night.

Having to stay out until the wee hours,
I ended up sleeping all day
on my mattress of cardboard boxes,
sheltered a little by the doorway of a building.
People no longer pay attention to me.
I don't even know if they know that
there is someone dozing under
that pile of old clothes.
But, after all, I am a bear.
And a bear in the city —
there's no such thing.

When people do notice me, they make a face.
I tell myself that I must not smell very good.
It's true that it's been a long time since I've bathed,
but a bear smells like a bear — that's just how it is.
All they have to do is plug their noses . . .

On one particular morning,
I was feeling like a grumpy old bear.
I was sitting on my cardboard boxes staring aimlessly.
I no longer even paid attention to the people who passed by
without even glancing at me. I was lost in my thoughts,
grumbling about my poor bear life,
when a small voice caught my attention:
"Why do you look so sad?"

Speechless, I raised my head to find
a little girl looking at me.
It was the first time in ages that
someone had spoken to me.
"Are you sad because you smell bad?"
I remembered the woman at the bakery
who had been so afraid, and I just shook my head "no."
The girl gave a little smile and came closer.
"You look like a teddy bear.
But a teddy bear never looks that sad."

I didn't get a chance to answer.
Her father grabbed her by the hand,
and they hurried away. He seemed to be
explaining something to her with big gestures.
At the end of the street, the little girl
turned her head toward me, and on her lips
I read: "See you tomorrow."

The next day, when they came back, I was clean as a raccoon, my fur brushed and shiny. I had straightened up my pile of boxes — I didn't want to make a bad impression. The girl smiled at me, came up to me, and whispered in the hollow of my ear: "Hello, teddy bear."

That warmed my heart as if all of those cold winters spent on this sidewalk had never happened. Then she continued skipping along on her way to school. And when she turned the corner, she gave me a little wave.

Today, like every morning, I wait for her. I know that when she arrives, my heart will leap in my chest, and suddenly my life will feel brighter, like when the sun breaks through the clouds.

I may only be a bear lost in the city, but I am a teddy bear.

And that's no small thing!

JEAN-FRANÇOIS DUMONT is a French author and illustrator who has created many stories for children, including *The Chickens Build a Wall* and *The Sheep Go on Strike* (both Eerdmans), as well as *A Blue So Blue*, winner of the Prix Saint-Exupéry, an award given yearly to the best illustrated picture book in France.

First published in the United States in 2015 by
Eerdmans Books for Young Readers,
an imprint of Wm. B. Eerdmans Publishing Co.
2140 Oak Industrial Dr. NE
Grand Rapids, Michigan 49505
P.O. Box 163, Cambridge CB3 9PU U.K.

www.eerdmans.com/youngreaders

Originally published in France in 2010 under the title
Je Suis Un Ours
by Kaléidoscope, 11, rue de Sèvres, 75006 Paris, France
www.editions-kaleidoscope.com
Text and illustrations © 2010 Jean-François Dumont
© 2010 Kaléidoscope
This English edition © 2015 Eerdmans Books for Young Readers

Manufactured at Tien Wah Press in Malaysia

21 20 19 18 17 16 15   9 8 7 6 5 4 3 2 1

Library of Congress Cataloging-in-Publication Data

Dumont, Jean-François, 1959- author, illustrator.
[Je suis un ours. English]
I am a bear / written and illustrated by Jean-François Dumont ;
[translated by Leslie Mathews].
pages cm
Summary: A homeless bear living in a city has a hard time getting by,
but when a little girl makes friends with him, his life becomes brighter.
ISBN 978-0-8028-5447-6
[1. Bears — Fiction. 2. Homelessness — Fiction.]
I. Mathews, Leslie, translator. II. Title.
PZ7.D89367Iad 2015
[E] — dc23
2014048097

FSC
www.fsc.org
MIX
Paper from
responsible sources
FSC® C012700